CACTUS CREATURE

Happy Birthday,
Marcus!

love -
Mrs.Wong

CACTUS CREATURE

Written by
James Gelsey

A
LITTLE APPLE
PAPERBACK

SCHOLASTIC INC.

New York Toronto London Auckland Sydney
Mexico City New Delhi Hong Kong Buenos Aires

ISBN 0-439-56116-7

Designed by Louise Bova

12 11 10 9 8 7 6 5 4 3   7 8 9/0

Special thanks to Duendes del Sur for cover and interior illustrations.
Printed in the U.S.A.
First printing, May 2005

Chapter 1

The Mystery Machine rolled down the desert highway, racing the tumbleweeds. The sun beat down on the enormous rock formations that dotted the sandy landscape.

"Like, where's the chocolate?" asked Shaggy as he climbed into the front seat.

"Rand rice cream?" Scooby added. He joined Shaggy up front and lay across everyone's laps.

"Watch it, you two!" Daphne cried. "This front seat was not designed for four people."

"Rand a rog," Scooby corrected.

As Fred turned the steering wheel, his hand knocked Scooby in the head.

"Rouch!" Scooby cried.

"Sorry, Scooby, but you're kind of in my way," Fred said.

"And mine," Daphne said.

"And mine," Velma echoed.

"Fine, we know when we're not wanted," Shaggy said. "Come on, Scooby, let's go wait for dessert in the back."

As Shaggy and Scooby climbed back over the front seat, Scooby's tail covered Fred's eyes.

"Scooby! I can't see!" Fred yelled, slamming on the brakes. Everyone flew forward as the Mystery Machine came to a sudden stop. The gang untangled themselves, and Fred began driving again.

"What has gotten into you two?" Daphne asked Shaggy and Scooby.

"Sorry, Daph, but we can't help it," Shaggy said. "We're just so excited about the food!"

Velma looked puzzled. "I know you two are always hungry," she said. "But what food are you talking about?"

"Ressert!" Scooby barked.

"Scooby, we're going to a video shoot," Velma explained. "Not a restaurant."

Shaggy laughed. "Like, we know that, Velma," he said. "But Scooby and I checked the map, and we saw what you circled." He picked up the map and showed it to Velma and Daphne. "See, the Rancho Chimichanga Dessert." He pointed. "And everyone knows that a Rancho Chimichanga Dessert contains three layers of chocolate, three layers of ice cream, and three layers of absolute delicious yumminess smothered in whipped cream and hot fudge and bananas!"

Daphne shook her head in disbelief. "Shaggy, Rancho Chimichanga is a desert," she said. "*Desert*, not dessert. We're going to a video shoot in the desert."

Shaggy and Scooby took a moment to let this new information sink in.

"You mean there won't be any chocolate?" asked Shaggy.

"Ror rice cream?" asked Scooby.

Fred shook his head. "Fellas, that stuff wouldn't last five minutes in the desert sun," he said. "Sorry to disappoint you."

"If there's no dessert, then what's the big deal?" asked Shaggy.

Velma held up a compact disc.

"You see this CD?" she asked. "It contains some software and computer music files. I'm helping one of the band members with some computer trouble, so he invited us to the video shoot here in the desert."

Fred peered out the windshield. "Any sign of it, Velma?" he asked.

"According to the map, there should be a turnoff just ahead," she said.

5

Fred found the road and made a sharp turn. At the end of the dusty road, he saw a line of trailers.

"There it is!" Velma announced. "Next stop, our very first video shoot!"

Chapter 2

red pulled the van alongside one of the trailers and turned off the engine. As soon as he got out, Shaggy started pulling at his shirt collar.

"Oh, the heat!" Shaggy moaned. "Water! Water!"

Scooby-Doo pretended to faint and fell to the ground.

"Very funny, you two," Daphne said.

"We've got a cooler full of water bottles in the back of the van."

"Come on, let's go find the director," Fred said.

As Fred, Velma, and Daphne walked off, Shaggy and Scooby opened the back of the van. They each grabbed a bottle of water from the cooler and drank it in one gulp.

"Aaaaaahhhh," Shaggy said.

"Rereshing!" Scooby said.

"Now let's go see what this video thing is all about," Shaggy said. He slammed the van door shut. Shaggy noticed a tall cactus standing next to the van. It was almost as tall as Shaggy, with two rounded arms pointing up. Sharp quills ran up and down the entire plant.

"Like, I don't remember seeing a cactus here before," Shaggy remarked. "Do you, Scooby?"

Scooby shook his head.

"Oh, well, I guess we were so thirsty we

didn't notice," Shaggy said. "Let's go catch up to the others."

As they walked away from the van, they heard footsteps.  They turned and saw the cactus standing right behind them again. Suddenly, the cactus opened two angry dark eyes and a frightening mouth.

"GAAAAARRRRRR!" shouted the cactus.

"Run, Scooby!" Shaggy cried.

He and Scooby ran screaming until they crashed right into Velma, Daphne, and Fred.

"Felma! Vaphne! Dred!" Shaggy gasped, trying to catch his breath. "Mactus conster!"

"What?" exclaimed Fred, Daphne, and Velma together.

"Scooby and I were getting a drink when

this giant cactus showed up and started chasing us!" Shaggy said. "Show 'em, Scoob."

"Rike ris," Scooby said. He stood and raised his paws up like the cactus.

"Only the cactus was covered in needles instead of fur," Shaggy added.

"I think maybe the desert sun has started baking their brains," said a man standing next to Velma.

"No, they're always like this," Velma said. "Boys, this is O'N."

"Like, nice to meet you, Owen," Shaggy said.

"No, not Owen," the man said. "O'N. Each letter is separate. Now, Velma, do you have the CD? We can't shoot the video without the Trundles. And the Trundles can't play without the CD."

"The who-dles?" asked Shaggy.

"The Trundles," Fred said. "They had a number one album a few years ago."

"But haven't had a hit since," Daphne said.

"And if I don't shoot this video in the next twenty-four hours, the music company will drop the band and that will be the end of the Trundles," O'N explained.

Just then, a sound engineer passed by and mumbled, "That would be fine with me."

Chapter 3

O'N, the director, glared at the sound engineer.

"What was that, Otto?" he asked.

"Nothing," answered the sound engineer. Then he stopped and turned around. "No, it wasn't nothing." He marched back toward O'N and the gang. As he walked, the wires dangling from his utility belt knocked together and chimed slightly.

"I worked on the Trundles' first album," he said. "I spent countless hours in the recording studio with them. I worked just as hard as anyone, and what happened? They forgot to put my name in the credits! You can go through the liner notes with a fine-toothed comb and never find the name Otto Sorts mentioned once. Not once!"

As Otto gestured, the roll of green tape around his wrist came flying off. O'N ducked out of the way just in time.

"That was five years ago, Otto," O'N said. "Time to let it go."

"Yeah, yeah," Otto muttered. He picked up his tape and went on his way.

"Well, we've got a video to shoot," O'N said. "The band should be in their trailer. Bring them the CD while I get everything else ready."

O'N went about his business as the gang searched for the band's trailer. They heard loud music coming from a trailer with a tie-dyed paint job.

13

"This must be the place," Velma said, knocking on the door.

"Come on in, it's open!" a woman's voice called from inside.

The gang opened the door and stepped up into the trailer.

"Uh, Velma, are you sure we're in the right place?" Daphne asked.

The gang was surrounded by racks and racks of clothing. Shelves of wigs filled the far wall. In the middle of it all stood a tall woman with a tall pink-and-blue hairdo. She wore a pink flowered wraparound shirt and light green capri pants. When Daphne looked down, she saw the three-inch heels that gave the woman her height.

"Can I help you kids?" she asked.

"Sorry, we were looking for the Trundles," Velma said. "I guess we got the wrong trailer."

"No, honey, if you're looking for the Trundles, you got the right trailer," the woman said. "Like the saying goes, 'clothes make the band.' And this is where the band gets its clothes. I'm Charelle. Charelle Yucca, the band's wardrobe designer."

"Nice to meet you," Daphne said. "I'm Daphne. And this is Velma, Fred, Shaggy, and Scooby-Doo."

"And what brings you young people out to the middle of nowhere?" asked Charelle.

Velma explained that she was helping the band with their music software and computer problems. Charelle shook her head as she went back to work. She was putting some wire into a shirt hem to keep it stiff.

"Isn't it sad what music's coming to?" She frowned. "I've been in the business for more years than I care to remember. And music used to come from the heart. It came from the soul. It came from a lot of places, but it didn't come from computers, that's for sure."

She finished with the shirt and examined a green jumpsuit hanging next to it. She ripped a small piece of green tape from a roll and placed it over a tiny rip in the fabric.

"And don't think I don't know what I'm talking about," Charelle continued. "In my day, I used to write lyrics for songs. Then work started drying up, so I got into the wardrobe business. That's when the Trundles hired me. I think it's because they wanted to use my song ideas and lyrics. Of course, I could never prove anything, but there's a little voice inside me that believes to this day they stole some of my best work."

"That's terrible," Daphne said.

Charelle nodded. "I know, but let's face it, who'd ever believe a lowly wardrobe lady? No, the Trundles will get theirs, just you wait." Charelle turned her attention back to her clothing. "Sorry, kids, but I have to finish getting these things ready for the video shoot," she said. "The band's in the white trailer with the green stripe on it."

The gang thanked Charelle and left the wardrobe trailer.

"Come on, fellas," Daphne said. "Shaggy? Scooby-Doo?"

Fred, Daphne, and Velma looked around and saw that Shaggy and Scooby were missing.

Chapter 4

There was no sign of Shaggy or Scooby anywhere.

"Great!" Fred said. "Now where are they?"

"Surprise!" Shaggy said, jumping out in front of them. "Ms. Yucca said we could try these on. How do we look?"

Shaggy wore big sunglasses, a long pink feathery coat, and shiny blue boots. Scooby wore a black leather jacket and black leather

19

pants. He sported a purple Mohawk on his head.

Fred, Daphne, and Velma had to laugh.

"You two look great!" Daphne said. "It's too bad you don't have any talent, otherwise you'd make great rock stars."

"Talent?" said a woman standing next to the trailer. "To be a rock star, all you need to have is *no* talent. Just look at the Trundles!" The woman laughed. "Oh, I'm only

kidding — a little. The name's Simmy Brackish," she said, holding out her hand. As Daphne shook it, she noticed a couple of green bandages on Simmy's fingers.

"Pleased to meet you, Ms. Brackish," Daphne said. "Are you working on the video, also?"

"I'm a botanist by training," Simmy said. "But I've become a set decorator. It's my job to find the plants that the directors use on their sets. For example, since we're going with a desert theme for this video shoot, I've had to find some natural desert-type plants for the background."

"Like a cactus?" asked Velma.

"Yes, but the cactus family is pretty large," Simmy said. "So I have to be able to offer the director a choice between golden

21

barrel, bishop's hat, teddy bear cholla, giant saguaro, ocotillo, and things like that."

"Jeepers, I never realized there were so many types of cacti," Daphne said.

"Like, how about the famous chasing cactus?" Shaggy asked.

"The what?" Simmy asked.

"Never mind," Fred said. "Shaggy and Scooby think they were chased by a cactus when we got here."

Simmy thought for a moment. "No, I can't say I recall any kind of walking cactus. It's possible, though, that one became detached from its roots and was blown along by the wind."

"Man, I feel like a baked potato wrapped in tinfoil," Shaggy said. "These costumes are hot!"

"Reah, ret's get ranged," Scooby said.

"Good idea, Scooby," Shaggy said. "Like, we'll be back in a minute."

Shaggy and Scooby stepped up into the nearest trailer.

"Wait, that's the cactus room!" Simmy called, but it was too late. Shaggy and Scooby climbed inside. A moment later, they jumped out.

"Sorry, fellas, but that room is wall-to-wall cactus," Simmy said. "I needed to bring a whole bunch of samples because I never know what O'N is going to want. Sometimes he changes his mind three times in five minutes."

"So you've worked with O'N before?" Velma asked. "What about the Trundles?"

"This is my first gig with the Trundles," Simmy answered. "I've done most of my video work with the Fuzzy Funk Express."

"You've worked with the Fuzzy Funk Express?" Daphne gasped. "They're fantastic!"

Simmy put her finger up to her lips. She explained that the Fuzzy Funk Express had stolen away most of the Trundles' fans. "In fact," she added, "as soon as this shoot is over, I'm going to work on the Express' newest video. Just don't tell anyone, all right?"

Simmy climbed into the trailer and came out holding a large barrel cactus.

"Step aside, unless you want to become a human pincushion," she said. Simmy carried the cactus over to the set.

"You know, I still have to give the band the CD," Velma said. "And I have a hunch we're running out of time."

"What makes you say that?" asked Fred.

"Them!" Velma replied. She pointed to the four costumed band members leaving the wardrobe trailer.

"Like, follow that band!" Shaggy said.

24

Chapter 5

The gang followed the four band members to the stage. The stage was decorated with an assortment of plants, including several large cacti. Onstage, Otto Sorts was putting little green pieces of tape on the floor to mark where the band members should stand.

"Try to hit your marks," Otto reminded the band members as he left. "Otherwise the microphones may not pick up your voices properly."

"Vomitina!" Velma called. One of the band members turned around.

"Velma!" She smiled. "Great to see you. Just in time, too! Do you have the CD?"

Velma produced the CD and handed it to Vomitina.

"Thanks!" she said. "I was getting worried, but I knew you'd never let us down."

Vomitina followed the three other band members onto the stage. She sat down behind a large electronic keyboard. She popped the CD into the drive and checked the monitor mounted over the keyboard.

"The software is loading . . . loading . . . loading . . . and is loaded!" she announced. "Everything's looking good, thanks to Velma!"

The other band members thanked Velma as they took their places.

"It was nothing, really," Velma began. "Just a couple of minor problems in the source code of the software that prevented the dynamics of the music from being digitized properly."

"All right, people!" O'N announced. "Let's do a quick sound check and then get this video in the can!"

Vomitina removed Velma's CD and inserted it into the keyboard's computer.

"Ready, mates?" she asked the other band members. They nodded and began playing.

Suddenly, it seemed like the entire desert exploded in song.

"CUT! CUT! HOLD IT!" O'N shouted. The band stopped just as suddenly as they started. "That should be enough for Otto to set his levels. Now remember, this song is about life. It's about fighting the odds and overcoming adversity. It's about —"

"Ractus!" Scooby cried.

"Yes, yes, the cactus is the metaphor for life in a hot, empty place," O'N agreed. "But it's also about —"

"Zoinks! Cactus!" Shaggy shrieked.

"Yes, the cactus, but there's much, much more to this song," O'N continued, ignoring them. "There's also —"

"CACTUS MONSTER!" Fred, Daphne, and Velma yelled. O'N spun around and saw a giant cactus monster running across the stage. The creature looked just like the one Shaggy and Scooby had described earlier.

28

The monster shot little spiny needles into the air, forcing the band members to dive out of the way. The monster reached Vomitina's computer and piano keyboard. With one flick of its cactuslike hand, the monster opened the CD drive and grabbed the CD from inside.

"NO MORE MUSIC!" the monster threatened. "NO MORE MUSIC!" The monster shot some more quills at the instruments and then ran off the stage and into the desert.

"Man, I told you we saw a walking cactus!" Shaggy said.

"Well, let's get it!" Fred said. Everyone started after the cactus but had to stop. The monster had left behind a massive pile of cactus quills that were too pointy and too dangerous to cross safely.

"Oh, no!" cried Vomitina. "That cactus weirdo stole the CD. It's got all of our music on it!"

"All right, we'll use the backup for the video," O'N said. "Where is it?"

"We don't have one," Vomitina said.

O'N stared at her in disbelief. "You don't have one?"

"We didn't have time to make one," Vomitina said. "We needed Velma to get here with the software patch to fix the program. Once we did that, it was time to start."

"You mean that without the CD there's no video?" asked Daphne.

"And without the video there's no chance of a comeback," O'N said. "We either find that monster and get that CD or say good-bye to the Trundles."

Fred, Daphne, and Velma looked at one another and nodded.

"Don't worry," Fred said. "Mystery, Inc. is on the case!"

Chapter 6

If we're going to solve this mystery, we should see where this trail of quills leads," Fred said. He pointed to the sprinkling of cactus quills that spread out before them like a long carpet.

The gang began walking, keeping their eyes open for anything suspicious.

"Ooo! Ouch! Rikes!" Scooby cried, hopping around on different feet.

"Careful, Scoob," Shaggy said. "Like, don't walk on the trail, walk around it."

Scooby sat down on a rock and blew on his feet. Daphne came over and pulled some quills from his paws.

"Aaaaaaaahhhhhhh," Scooby sighed. Then he gave Daphne a great big lick.

"Don't mention it, Scooby." She laughed, wiping her face.

As he stood up, Scooby felt something on his tail. He tried to flick it off, but it was still there. He looked over his shoulder and saw something green hanging on his tail.

"Srake! Srake!" he cried, jumping up and down and all around.

"Where's the snake? Where? Where?" Shaggy asked, jumping onto a large rock. Scooby pointed behind himself.

"Hold still, Scooby," Velma said.

"That's no snake," Fred said. "That's just a piece of green tape."

"Green tape? That's odd," Daphne said. "Why would there be a piece of green tape out here in the middle of nowhere?"

"I have a hunch our cactus monster dropped it," Velma said.

"Which tells me that this cactus monster isn't a real monster after all," Fred continued. "So whoever is dressed up like the monster must have used green tape."

"Like Otto the sound engineer," Daphne said. "He was marking the stage."

"And I remember Charelle Yucca used it for the costumes," Velma said.

"And that botanist even had some on her fingers when I shook her hand," Daphne recalled.

"And they each seemed to have a reason for wanting to keep the Trundles from succeeding," Fred said. "I'd say this first clue is pretty important. But it's not enough."

"Fred's right," Velma agreed. "We'd better split up to cover more ground."

Fred and Daphne decided to explore the outlying areas a bit more. Velma, Shaggy, and Scooby headed back to the trailers to look for clues.

"And remember, you two, no fooling around," Velma said. "We need to find more clues, and fast."

"No prob-lem-o," Shaggy said. "Come on, Scooby, I remember one trailer back there that looked very suspicious. We'll catch up with you in a little bit, Velma."

Velma watched Shaggy and Scooby walk down the row of trailers.

"Hmmm, that's very unlike them," she said to herself. "But I'd better spend my time looking for clues instead of worrying about Shaggy and Scooby."

Meanwhile, as Shaggy and Scooby kept walking, Shaggy kept looking over his shoulder.

"Great, Velma's gone!" Shaggy said. "Remember how I said a trailer looked very suspicious, Scoob?"

"Rh-huh." Scooby nodded.

"I really meant to say the trailer *smelled* very suspicious," Shaggy said. "And this is it. The food trailer!"

Shaggy and Scooby stepped up into the trailer. It was wall-to-wall food.

"Man, look at this place! It's a buffet on wheels!" Shaggy cried. "Forget the Mystery Machine. This is the kind of van I'm going to drive from now on!"

Shaggy and Scooby dove headfirst into the buffet and stuffed their faces.

"Man, these rock stars really know how to live," Shaggy said. "It's a wonder they get any music done at all."

As they ate, they felt the trailer begin to tilt. Food started sliding off the table and across the floor. Soon Shaggy and Scooby were sliding across the floor.

"Hold on, Scooby," Shaggy cried. He and Scooby pushed the door open and managed to throw themselves out of the trailer. They landed on their backs in a cloud of dust and sand. When it cleared, they noticed the trailer had been jacked up on one side. Then they looked straight up in the air.

"Say, doesn't that cloud look a little like the cactus monster?" Shaggy asked.

"Rit ris ruh ractus ronster!" Scooby cried. "RUN!"

Chapter 7

Shaggy and Scooby jumped up and ran as fast as they could. They turned the corner and headed for the wardrobe trailer. The door opened and out popped Velma.

"Rikes!" Scooby cried.

"Quick, back inside, Velma!" Shaggy shouted. He and Scooby pushed Velma back up into the trailer and slammed the door. The two of them barricaded the door with a rack of clothes and then hid under the ironing board.

"What's going on?" Velma asked.

"That cactus monster is after us," Shaggy whimpered.

There was a knock at the door. The handle jiggled.

"Man, I'm too young to be eaten by a cactus!" moaned Shaggy.

The door opened and Shaggy and Scooby shut their eyes.

"Velma? Is that you?" Fred asked. "Daphne and I thought we saw you come in here with Shaggy and Scooby."

Velma moved the clothes rack out of the way. She motioned to the ironing board. Shaggy and Scooby opened their eyes and smiled.

"It seems like these

two found trouble again," Velma said. "They said the monster chased them."

"All the way from the food trailer to here," Shaggy said.

"The food trailer?" Velma repeated. "Was that the suspicious place you had to check out?"

Shaggy and Scooby smiled sheepishly.

"Never mind that," Fred said. "Take a look at what we found in that pile of quills." He held out his hand and showed Velma a piece of coiled wire.

"That's an odd and very unnatural shape for a cactus quill," Velma stated.

"But it's not such an odd shape for something a person could use for their job," Daphne added.

Fred and Velma nodded.

"We're definitely on the right track," Fred said. "We just need one more clue to figure out this mystery."

41

"We're not going to find it in here, that's for sure," Velma said.

"Let's go, Scooby," Daphne said. "You, too, Shaggy. We still need your help to get this thing solved."

Shaggy stood up and bumped his head on the underside of the ironing board. Scooby walked carefully out from beneath it.

"Where to?" asked Daphne.

"I say we head back to the stage," Velma said. "I didn't have a chance to give it another look."

The gang left the wardrobe trailer and walked back to the stage. Everything was pretty much as they had left it. Except for one thing.

"All of the plants are gone!" Daphne noticed.

"Man, is that creepy or what?" Shaggy asked. "I hope they didn't, like, come to life or anything."

"No, they didn't come to life," O'N said, sitting off to the side. "I had a couple of stage-hands bring them all back to the plant trailer. No sense wasting money on plants if we're not doing the video shoot. If you need me, I'll be in my trailer."

"That explains what you saw, Shaggy," Fred said. "It was probably one of the stagehands returning a cactus to the plant trailer."

"I don't know, Fred, this cactus seemed awfully big," Shaggy said. "Sort of like that one over there."

Shaggy pointed to a lone cactus standing in the middle of the stage.

"Jinkies, that wasn't there a minute ago," Velma exclaimed.

"And didn't O'N say he had all the plants returned to the trailer?" Daphne asked.

"Oh, man, not again," Shaggy moaned.

Suddenly, the cactus sprang to life and

chased the gang off the stage
with a mighty roar. Everyone
ran off in different direc-
tions, and the monster dis-
appeared into the desert.

A few minutes later, Fred,
Velma, and Daphne came back
to the stage. Shaggy and Scooby
followed.

"Man, that was close," Fred said.

"A little too close," Daphne agreed. "Say,
what's this?"

She noticed a long black cable on the
ground. She picked it up and pulled it in. At
the end dangled a pair of headphones.

"Whatever you do, don't put those on,"
Velma said, examining them closely.

"Why not?" Shaggy asked. "They look
like regular old headphones to me."

"They've got little prickly quills on the
earpieces," Velma said. "It looks to me like it's

44

time to stick this cactus monster into jail where it belongs."

"Velma's right, everyone," Fred said. "Shaggy, Scooby, how would you two like to become rock stars?"

Chapter 8

Scooby's eyes lit up.

"Reah, rock rars!" he said happily.

"You and Shaggy are going to star in your very own music video," Fred continued. "I'm going to speak to O'N and get his help setting it up. Velma, you'll need to operate the keyboard computer. And Daphne, go to the wardrobe trailer and get as much of the heaviest fabric as you can find."

"Let's rock and roll, pal," Shaggy said. He and Scooby found their costumes from before and put them on. They raced back to the stage and each grabbed a guitar. Velma sat at the keyboard and turned on the computer.

"Velma, you've got to get with the groove," Shaggy said. "Here."

He put his oversized sunglasses on Velma. Scooby gave her his purple Mohawk.

"Much better," Shaggy said.

Fred returned with O'N as Daphne came over with the fabric.

"And then Daphne and I will run onto the stage and wrap the monster up in the fabric she found," Fred said to O'N.

"Sounds crazy, but I'll try anything," O'N said. "Let me know when to start." He took his position behind the camera.

"Uh, Fred-o, can we have a word?" asked Shaggy. "You mentioned that you and Daphne will capture the monster when it runs onto the stage. The thing is that, like, me and Scooby will be on the stage."

"That's right," Fred said. "You're the bait."

"Oh, the bait," Shaggy said. "Did Scooby or I ever mention that we're allergic to bait?"

"Allergic?" asked Fred.

"Some people get runny noses," Shaggy explained. "But when we're around monsters, we get runny feet. So we'll just wait until monster season is over. See ya!"

"Hold on, you two," Daphne said. "We can't do this without you."

"How do you know if you never tried?" asked Shaggy.

"Come on, Scooby, how about it?" asked Velma. "Will you help us for a Scooby Snack?"

Scooby thought and then shook his head. "Ruh-uh!"

"How about two Scooby Snacks?" asked Daphne.

Scooby tried to remain steadfast, but his hunger was mightier than his fear.

"Rokay!" he barked. Velma and Daphne each tossed Scooby a treat. He gobbled them down and then picked up his guitar.

"Rit it!" he cheered.

"That's my line!" Vomitina called from the side of the stage. "You two look great. Even you, Velma!"

"Places, everyone!" O'N shouted. "And . . . action!"

Velma pushed a button on the keyboard and music exploded from the speakers all over the stage. Shaggy and Scooby pretended to play. Even Velma got into it. Sure enough, a menacing roar filled the stage. The cactus monster had returned!

"Zoinks! He's here, Scooby!" Shaggy cried.

"Now!" Fred yelled. He and Daphne ran onto the stage, spreading out the material. "Duck, fellas!"

Scooby heard Fred and managed to get out of the way. Unfortunately, so did the cactus monster. Shaggy, however, didn't, and found himself wrapped up in the fabric. His guitar stuck out and, as he spun around, it knocked Fred and Daphne into the backdrop.

The cactus monster got up and ran toward Velma. Scooby put out his guitar and tripped the monster. Velma jumped off the stage just in time. The cactus creature fell to the ground. Vomitina and O'N ran over, grabbed the microphone cables, and wrapped up the monster.

Chapter 9

Within a few minutes, everyone managed to pull themselves together. They stood around the cactus monster, who was tied up on the ground.

"Well, who'd like to do the honors?" asked Fred.

"I would," Vomitina said. She reached over and realized there were too many quills on the costume to grab it safely.

"Here, use this," Daphne said. She handed her a piece of the fabric. Vomitina wrapped it around her hand and grabbed the cactus monster's head. With a firm yank, the costume came undone.

"Otto Sorts!" O'N said.

"Just as we thought," Velma said.

"You did?" asked Vomitina. "How did you know?"

"Well, it wasn't easy at first," Daphne said.

"We knew that Otto, Charelle, and Simmy all had reasons for wanting the Trundles to fail. And the first clue we found confirmed that they were our suspects."

"That's right," Fred said. "The green tape we found reminded us of the kind of tape each of them used for different reasons."

"But then we found a piece of coiled wire beneath the pile of quills," Daphne continued.

"Once we realized that no real cactus would have something like that on it, we remembered that Charelle was using wire in one of the costumes," Velma said.

"And that Otto had some on his utility belt," Fred said.

"But it took the last clue to clinch it," Daphne said. "A pair of headphones that only a sound engineer would need."

Otto Sorts sneered at the gang. "I can't believe it," he snarled. "Everything was going perfectly. I had it all worked out. I was going to take that CD and cut my own album and get the rewards I deserved for all of my hard work."

"Speaking of the CD, where is it?" Vomitina asked.

Otto refused to tell, but Velma nodded knowingly.

"He hid it someplace he thought we'd never look," Velma said.

"Where?" asked O'N.

"In the plant trailer," Simmy Brackish said, walking over to everyone. She held the shiny disk in her hand.

"He must have seen the stagehands clearing the plants," Daphne said. "And he knew they were just going to be returned to the nursery. My guess is that he was going to get the CD later when no one was around."

"I can't thank you kids enough," O'N said.

"And I can't curse you kids enough," Otto

said. "Everything was perfect. Absolutely perfect. But then you meddlesome kids ruined everything. You and your good-for-nothing dog."

"Oh, I wouldn't say their dog is good for nothing," Vomitina said. "In fact, I'd say he's good for something. Take a look at this."

Vomitina pointed to the video monitor at

the side of the stage. O'N started the video player. The screen came to life with Shaggy, Scooby, and Velma pretending to be a rock-and-roll band.

"I think we have a new concept for the video," O'N announced.

"And some new music, too," Vomitina said. "Where did you get that song, Velma?"

"That? When I created the software patch for your music program, I had to make sure it worked," she explained. "I input some random notes and the program generated a song."

"Well, that stuff is out of this world,"

Vomitina said. "Can we use some of it in our video?"

"Sure," Velma said.

"But only if you use Scooby-Doo, too!" Shaggy added.

"Scooby-Dooby-Dooooo!" Scooby cheered as everyone burst into applause.

About the Author

As a boy, James Gelsey used to run home from school to watch the Scooby-Doo cartoons on television (only after finishing his homework). Today, he still enjoys watching them with his wife and two daughters. He also has a real dog named Scooby who loves nothing more than a good Scooby Snack!